Nana's Gift

Janette Oke

II•II•II•II•II•II•II•II•II•II•II•II•II•II•II•II

Nana's Gift

BETHANY HOUSE PUBLISHERS
MINNEAPOLIS, MINNESOTA 55438

Cover illustration by Jennifer Heyd Wharton.
Book insides designed by Sherry Paavola.
Illustrations by Hetty Mitchell.

Published by Bethany House Publishers
A Ministry of Bethany Fellowship, Inc.
11300 Hampshire Avenue South
Minneapolis, Minnesota 55438

Printed in the United States of America.

ISBN 1-55661-898-0

*Dedicated to my
children and grandchildren
in memory of their
great-grandmother and
great-great-grandmother
Violet Dell Ruggles
whose life taught much
about love and faith.*

JANETTE OKE was born in Champion, Alberta, during the Depression years, to a Canadian prairie farmer and his wife. She is a graduate of Mountain View Bible College in Didsbury, Alberta, where she met her husband, Edward. They were married in May of 1957 and went on to pastor churches in Indiana as well as Calgary and Edmonton, Canada.

The Okes have three sons and one daughter and are enjoying the addition of grandchildren to the family. Edward and Janette have both been active in their local church, serving various capacities as Sunday school teachers and board members. They make their home near Calgary, Alberta.

Books by Janette Oke

Contents

The Plan

The chiming of clocks having long since replaced the duties of a town crier, the mantel clock in the living room began its announcement. The man seated at the kitchen table, bent over the papers and the ledger scattered before him, lifted his head and counted without conscious thought. Twelve chimes. This time the last note signaled not just a new hour but a new year. Another year gone by. It seemed they passed so quickly. Much faster than when he was a younger man.

Not that he was old. Fifty-one was not old. But a long day in the fields wresting a living from the sometimes stubborn soil made him realize that he was slowing down. He didn't have the drive—the push—that he'd had in his younger years. The will was still there. But it was more determination than energy that now ran his days.

He sighed, then nodded as though in agreement, head tipped slightly, as the last stroke for the midnight hour faded. From now on, each minute ticked away by the mantel clock would already be spending the precious wealth of time in another year.

Had Lizzie heard the clock? Did she know that a new year had begun? Was she listening for his footsteps that would bring him to their bed?

It had been his little ritual ever since they had first married—this staying up to figure out accounts on the last evening of

the year. At first Lizzie had protested. New Year's Eve was a time for merriment. For celebration, she'd insisted. For looking back on the year past and being thankful for the good—and there had always been things to be thankful for—and reaching forward into the New Year, hoping that life would be just a little easier. That the good, through the grace of God, would outweigh the difficult. That was Lizzie's reasoning.

But Duncan had responded that this—this accounting—was his way of doing that. He didn't suppose that Lizzie understood. But as he went through the pile of bills and noted that he had somehow managed to pay them off one by one, though often with great difficulty and much perseverance, he was filled with such a sense of thankfulness and even peace that he worshiped—and, yes, celebrated—as he made the entries in the bulky worn book that he referred to as

the farm ledger. And because of the good-
ness of God in the past, he always had confidence as he faced the future. The year that
was just beginning.

He fastened the pile of paid bills together with a clip and deposited them in the
metal box that served as his bank. He did
not use the local financial institution. His
own system worked just fine. Everything was
kept in the worn metal box that had long
since lost most of its dark red paint from

many years of handling. Each compartment was carefully organized—paid accounts here, unpaid accounts there, change in the upper left corner, bills on the lower left. Then the ledger itself would be slightly curled, to make it fit, and tucked away on top. Everything was there. He knew at a glance just where his accounts stood.

And tonight. Tonight the accounts were all paid, the money for the next month set aside in the left-hand compartment, and there still was a small pile of bills and change left before him on the table.

He smiled as he reached for it. It would be added to his little stash. Even Lizzie, who knew all his secrets, did not know about the lower compartment in the metal box, nor of its contents. He had been carefully hoarding. Squirreling away a special fund little by little over the years that they had spent together.

The secret account had not grown as quickly as he would have liked. He had hoped to have enough saved by the time their twenty-fifth wedding anniversary arrived. But that had come and gone and he still was short. Now he was hoping for their thirtieth. But the pile of bills and coins was growing so slowly. If their finances did not improve, he feared that he might not meet *that* goal either. They had already celebrated their twenty-eighth, so he had only two more years to go. At one point this last year he had dared to think he could add a sizable amount at his New Year's Eve accounting. The crop had been good. There had been no unexpected medical expenses or machine repairs. But then a missionary had come to their church, and it had seemed right and good to contribute toward the funds that were needed to help the man get to the place of God's calling. Duncan had dipped

even deeper than he normally did in order to support the cause—so the pile for the year was small again.

Slowly he lifted the tray and set it aside. He reached in for the envelope that held his little hoard of bills and change. It was another yearly ritual, this counting of the secret account. A time of elation—and sorrow. For as much as he was thrilled with what he had been able to save toward his goal, he always felt a bit disheartened as he recalled the distance remaining.

It had all begun on their honeymoon. Lizzie had been so young then. Young and vibrant and beautiful. She was still beautiful in his eyes. Perhaps even more so. The appealing bounce and naivety had been replaced by a serenity and devotion. He loved his Lizzie. She had stood by him through the good and the bad. And their years together had held both. But Lizzie—

Lizzie had helped him to weather those years. Smiling through tears at the wonder of their firstborn. Nursing their children through childhood illnesses. Clinging to him at the graveside of their infant son. Beaming with each accomplishment of their five offspring. Taking into an already crowded household his aged father when he was left as a widower benumbed by grief. Looking radiant as the mother of three young brides. The years with Lizzie had been good years. Even the struggles and setbacks had been times of growing together.

But he had never forgotten their honeymoon. They had been walking. Window-shopping, Lizzie had called it. They passed window after window with Lizzie often stopping to ooh and ahh over this or that in a display. She seemed to take pleasure in looking at all the things she did not have. He could not really understand her little game.

It seemed to him at the time that she should feel some kind of sadness over the fact that she had married a simple farmer and would likely never have any of the fancy things that were drawing her exclamations. But Lizzie had not looked sad. Just enthusiastic and excited by life. There was no sign of longing in the dancing eyes. "Would you like that?" he had asked at one point as they stood together while she oohed over a gleaming enameled kitchen range. She looked startled by his question. "Why?" she responded innocently. "We already have a stove."

They had a stove. An old, worn-out blackened thing that had been his grand-mother's.

But that was Lizzie. She didn't have a self-centered or coveting bone in her body. And that was when he decided. Someday, as soon as he could manage it, he'd get her

something really special. Something that she could be proud to own. Something that would speak of her true worth—and his deep love.

At the time he was sure it would take only a few years to save the money needed. Five, if things went well. Maybe ten. Then he would look for that special something. Some object that Lizzie could treasure.

But the children came, one by one, and there were tough years with scant crops. Lizzie never complained. The years rolled by, and she still did not have pretty things—nice things. But she was content to work along with him, smiling her encouragement, silently willing her strength when the load got especially heavy. Unaware of the hidden secret in the metal box.

He stirred himself from his reverie and added the year's small savings to the pile and placed it tenderly back in the envelope. Not

this year. He was still quite a few dollars short. But if God was pleased to grant them two good years, perhaps he would be able to make that thirtieth anniversary.

Gifts

e knew—had known for some time now—what the gift would be. He had been walking by Sam's Fine Gifts one day when he spied it in the display window. A string of perfectly formed pearls. He stood and gazed at the pearls for a long time, thinking about the story that Jesus told of the pearl of great price and the man who had sold everything to purchase it. Why would anyone want a pearl that badly? he asked himself silently. It didn't make any sense. Selling all one had—

good farmland—to purchase pearls. Foolish idea.

But he couldn't get the pearls from his mind. And then one day as he was milking, leaning his forehead against the warm side of Daisy the Holstein cow, it suddenly came to him that maybe Lizzie *would* understand. Maybe the string of pearls was just the right gift for her. The more he thought about it, the more the idea grew on him.

He walked by that window dozens of times before he got up the nerve to go in. "How much is that string of pearls in your window?" he had casually asked Sam. He was stunned at the answer and left the shop with his head spinning. It was impossible. It was ridiculous. Why, a man could purchase... But the idea wouldn't go away. These pearls were special. The price told him that. He remembered joking to himself that he sure hoped he wouldn't have to "sell

all that he had" to make the purchase. He chuckled inwardly and wondered if the farm would be worth as much as the pearls.

Months passed. He kept his eye on the string of pearls, fearful that someone else would buy them before he had saved enough.

At last he ambled into Sam's again.

"See you still have those pearls," he commented in what he hoped was an offhand manner.

Sam shook his head. "Shouldn't have brought them in," he said, and his shoulders drooped. "Not much call for pearls in these parts. Times have been hard. Folks need to use their money for more sensible things."

Duncan nodded and pretended to be studying a display of gold wedding bands.

"Maybe you need to mark 'em down some," he observed, tipping his head slightly to try to catch a bit of the light from the

window on the display case.

"Pearls aren't items that go on sale much," Sam had responded. "And even if I did mark them down a bit, they'd still be too rich for the pockets of folks around here."

Duncan nodded again, took one more look at the plain gold bands, and left the store with a polite farewell and a sinking heart.

Several months passed before he headed for the store again. This time he was determined that the pearls would be Lizzie's. His heart beat nervously when he noticed they were no longer in the window. He shuffled slightly as he spoke to Sam. "See you've sold the pearls."

But Sam shook his head. "Took them from the window and put them in the vault," he replied. "No sale for them anyway, and sitting out like that isn't good for them."

Duncan sucked in his breath, relief

washing over him. Lizzie's pearls were still safe. He steadied himself and spoke slowly, carefully. "Been thinking," he began. "Those pearls would look mighty nice with Lizzie's blue Sunday dress."

He flushed after the remark. That was a silly thing to say. By the time he saved enough to purchase the pearls, Lizzie's present Sunday dress would be a thing of the past.

He straightened then and looked Sam directly in the eyes. "What I'm saying is, I'd like to buy Lizzie the pearls. But I don't have the funds saved up—just yet. I was wondering if you could—sort of—hold them until I get the money together."

Sam looked startled, but at length he nodded, and eventually even smiled in relief. He was pleased to be finding a sale for his ill-advised investment.

Quickly the businessman in Sam turned

to longtime friend. "Look, Duncan," he said, clearing his throat. "That's a...a lot of money...when times are tough. I—if you'd like—I can order in another string. One that isn't so...so expensive."

Duncan must have looked puzzled. He had no idea that one could get pearls that were less expensive. Sam had already told him they were not an item that went on sale as a rule.

"Pearls come in different quality. Different color," Sam had gone on to explain. "That string—well it's top quality. I never should have brought it in. At the time it—well—there was that banker who liked to spend money, and then everyone round these parts was talking mining. If we'd had a strike here the way it looked like we might for a while—I guess greed sort of... Well, anyway, I can get you another."

But Duncan quickly cut in. He wouldn't

even think of getting Lizzie pearls that were inferior.

"These are just fine," he stated with finality. "It'll just take a bit longer, that's all."

"They should be restrung," Sam observed in knowledgeable fashion.

"Restrung?"

Sam then went through a lengthy explanation of the worth of each pearl and how one had to use care in ensuring that the string would never break, thus placing any one of the costly pearls in danger. Duncan caught very little of the explanation but was relieved when Sam ended by saying that he would hold the pearls, and when the time came for purchase he'd care for the cost of restringing himself. With the matter settled, Duncan laid out his small hoard of money as the down payment, and the pearls were secured in the vault for Lizzie. Duncan left

the store with a feeling of exhilaration. Now all he had to do was to save up the rest of the money.

But he'd had no idea how long that would take and at such great difficulty.

Slowly the years had ticked by. Now and then he dropped in to Sam's to lay a bit more money on the counter and sheepishly assure him that he was still saving toward the pearls. Sam had been good about it. Duncan had to admit that. But the man must have had his doubts whether the final sale would ever take place.

As the mantel clock chimed twelve fifteen, Duncan's thoughts were jerked back to the present. He fingered the envelope as he tucked it safely in its sheltered spot. Two more years. Would that really be enough?

Lizzie

Lizzie stirred, one hand reaching out to the pillow beside her. It was empty—cool to her touch. Duncan had already left their bed.

Choring, her mind managed to reason. Reluctantly and slowly she began to untangle herself from the delights of sleep. Duncan, who always jumped out of bed with thoughts and feet racing, had often teased her through the years about her difficulty in waking with each new day. Even in her bemused state the remembrance of the teas-

ing brought a smile.

"Chores," she said aloud. "It seems that a body should be able to rest from chores for at least one day of a lifetime."

But today would not be the day. Today the chores would demand Duncan's time just as they had done every morning of their married life. It did not matter that today marked their thirtieth anniversary. Thirty years. That seemed like such a long, long, *short* time. She could hardly believe it. Had no way to really tally it. The years had sped by—and yet she was hard put to remember what life had been before Duncan.

They had been good years. Not easy years—but good. She smiled again as she thought of their two manly sons and three grown daughters. They were all married now. All settled and on their own. The thought brought tears to her eyes. She was proud of each one and happy to release them—but it

was lonely at times. She missed them. Missed the noise and confusion of a bustling household. Missed the teasing and coaxing and even the testing of parental boundaries.

But the new kind of relationship with their children brought blessings as well. Stella was hosting the anniversary dinner. Lizzie knew that Jewel and Addie would help, and Luke's Mary and John's Cecily would also give a hand. It was nice to just relax and look forward to the special time with all the family. She curled up and prepared to enjoy just a few more moments reflecting as she snuggled in the warmth of the cozy comforter.

They were grandparents now. They had thought they were prepared for it, but they had both been caught off guard by the wonder of grandchildren. There was something so deeply profound—so entrancing about holding a grandchild. It was so unlike par-

enting. Almost spiritual in nature. The little bundles in your arms seemed to mesmerize you even before they managed that first smile. Four of them—and Addie about to add another to the family circle. Lizzie loved watching her grandchildren grow and develop, but she had missed having a soft, sweet-smelling baby in her arms to cuddle and coo. Lizzie found herself hardly able to wait for the new arrival.

She stretched again and let her eyes open fully and glanced about the room from where their bed stood. It needed freshening. She had hoped there would be egg money to buy new paper, new curtains, some paint for the woodwork, but—maybe next year. There were always so many places for the money to go.

But she was blessed. No family member had been ill. There had been no major catastrophes. She thought of the Hills who had

lost their home to fire. The Parkers whose young grandson had died in a drowning accident. Mr. Hedge who had suffered a stroke. Others around them had been hit with sorrow. Yes. They had been blessed. It truly had been another good year.

A little prayer of thanks formed on her lips as she stretched her foot to the rag rug by her bed. She was looking forward to the day.

Duncan chafed as he pitched hay to the cows. It hadn't happened. He still was unable to claim Lizzie's pearls. There was a sick, gnawing feeling in the pit of his stomach as he thought about his visit to see Sam. The man had been gracious, but he must have been disappointed too. Duncan was sure that Sam needed that sale. The drought

was as hard on shopkeepers as it was on farmers.

He had almost had enough. Had thought surely he would have enough—and then their neighbors, the Hills, had lost their home—everything—to fire. It didn't seem right to squirrel the money away when the needy family didn't even have clothes to dress their three young children.

He thought of the small gift he had purchased for the special anniversary. A new gas iron. It didn't seem appropriate for a woman like Lizzie. It was true that he'd caught her eyeing them at the local hardware—but it wasn't the gift that he really wished to be giving.

He pitched another forkful of hay with added force, scattering it over the necks of the yearlings instead of placing it in the manger. He chastised himself and settled in to controlled feeding. No use wasting good

hay just because he was feeling peeved with himself.

There was always next year.

Anniversaries

"Happy anniversary." Duncan tried a relaxed smile as he handed Lizzie the small, carefully wrapped package. He was so tight with tension that even his face muscles would not work right. He wondered if he looked as stiff as he felt.

She seemed not to notice. She accepted the package with her usual smile and passed her gift to him.

"Whose turn is it to go first?" she asked.

He felt the agitation increase.

They always took turns—year by year. But this year he did not wish to wait. He had waited long enough. Thirty-six years. Thirty-six years was long enough for a man to hold himself in check—to build up a full head of impatience without adding on more minutes of traditional turns.

But Lizzie was not to be rushed. "Let's see," she was calculating. "This is an even year. I started at one—odd. Yours have been the even years. So it is your turn."

With controlled effort he swallowed his petulance and quickly ripped the paper from the package—rather a heavy one—she had given to him. It was a new crescent wrench—one he had been admiring—but how had Lizzie known?

He should have responded with enthusiasm. He wanted to—but he could not think—could not speak. He gave Lizzie a cursory nod and managed to mumble some-

thing about it being just what he wanted, forced a smile, then encouragingly nodded again at the gift in her hand.

She finally began to carefully undo the wrappings. It was maddening, how painstakingly she went about it. His heart pounded more radically than when Lizzie was delivering their first child.

"Oh, what a beautiful box!" Lizzie exclaimed, her fingers caressing the blue velvet over and over.

Duncan felt ready to explode. "Open it," he said, his voice sounding forced. Choked.

But her fingers continued to stroke the exterior until he was tempted to snatch the box from her and jerk it open to expose the gift inside.

At length she lifted the lid and peeked in. A gasp followed. He watched her carefully and saw the wonder that filled her eyes.

"They're beautiful," she whispered, open-

ing the box fully. "They...they look...so real."

He could contain himself no longer. He took the blue box from her hands and tilted it slightly so the light from the window would fully illuminate the pearls. "They *are* real," he said with more force than he intended. "They have a warranty—or guarantee—or some such—and they've just been restrung, and Sam says—"

"Oh, Duncan." The words were softly spoken. They were so low that he could hardly hear them, and said in such a way that he could not interpret them.

❧

Lizzie's head was reeling. Whatever was he thinking? Spending all that money when there were so many things they needed? Practical things. Solid things. They didn't have that kind of money. What had he done?

She still hadn't gathered enough money together to redo the bedroom. Where had he come up with a sum for the likes of pearls?

Then her wild thoughts raced on. Perhaps they had been bought on credit. But Duncan had never believed in such purchases. "We must pay as we go," he had insisted year after difficult year. "If we can't keep up, how can we hope to catch up?" But he must have thrown aside his reserve and borrowed the funds. Lizzie was sure that Duncan had no other way to get money for such a sizable purchase. Surely he hadn't mortgaged the farm. Would they spend the rest of their lifetime paying off a string of pearls? Surely... surely...

With moist eyes she lifted her face to Duncan's. "They are beautiful—" she began, wondering just how to say the words that she must say. That the pearls were a lovely gesture—that she appreciated the sweet thought and would treasure the fact that she would always be able to say she had once owned a wonderfully authentic string of pearls—but they must go back. They must.

And then she saw his eyes.

Duncan had always been so easy for her to read. And now she read eagerness. Almost uncontrolled. And pride. He looked about to burst. And love—so much love it brimmed over and spilled into the drabness of the room, making even the faded wallpaper take on a new glow.

And she knew—instantly—that to reject his gift would cause him deep, wrenching pain. She could never do that. Never.

"They are beautiful," she said again, and this time her voice was trembling because the tears were beginning to flow.

He laid aside the velvet box and held her. Held her with more strength than when she had been a new bride. With more tenderness

than he had held her when they lost their infant son. With more love than she thought was possible for a man and a woman to share. And she wept. With joy. With wonder. And even with uncertainty. But mostly with love for the man she had married.

She would ask no questions. Have no doubts. She would wear her pearls with pride—and smile her thanks each time she looked at the man who had given them.

They would look lovely with her emerald Sunday dress.

"I had wanted you to have them earlier," he whispered into her hair. "A sort of—legacy thing. I wanted the girls to...to each be able to wear them on their wedding day. You know. Mama's pearls. Something special."

His voice sounded so apologetic, as though he had let her down. Let his girls down. Her arms tightened around his neck.

"But it took this long—" He stopped and

swallowed. "Took longer than I intended to save up the money," he finished, his voice taking on a husky sound.

The words reached her ears, but it took her some time to sort through the meaning. Save up the money? When she finally understood she almost went limp in his arms. Relief washed all over her. She forgot the needed wallpaper, the paint, the curtains. The pearls were paid for. There was no debt to face. Duncan had somehow managed over the years to save enough for this elaborate— this very special gift.

By the time she pushed back to look up into his face, her smile was genuine. Radiant. "We have granddaughters," she said with pleasure. "We'll let them wear Grandma's pearls."

Weddings

One by one they married. One by one the gowns were graced by Grandma's pearls. All five of them. Blushing brides, with different tastes and different dresses and much different young men nervously waiting at the altar. The one constant was the string of pearls—pearls religiously restrung as needed, just as Sam had long ago dictated.

Then there was a lull. Another generation had become homemakers. New babies began to fill new cradles. Small voices clam-

ored for the attention of great-grandparents.

There was something very special about great-grandchildren. There seemed to be more time to bask in the pleasure of their love. Duncan turned most of the farming over to John, who had built a house just down the road. John was quite able to care for the additional land with his fancy, big equipment that was now a part of farming. Duncan spent his time taking the great-grandsons fishing in the nearby stream and showing them how to whittle without nipping a finger. Lizzie baked cookies with the little girls and had afternoon tea parties on the wide veranda. And both she and Duncan faced each morning with deep contentment, secure in a way that went far beyond financial issues.

She stood alone long after the others had gone. John had voiced his concerns, but she had brushed them gently aside.

"I just need a few minutes—alone. Please," she pleaded. "If I don't have them now I'll just have to come back. You go. I'll come in a minute."

Reluctantly he had left her and joined the others at the waiting automobiles.

She stood and looked down at the mound before her, but she was not seeing the newly turned sod. Nor was she really seeing the polished mahogany, its top bedecked with sprays of deep red roses and shasta daisies. Duncan's favorite flowers. She looked beyond—and back. Back to the picture that she carried in her mind. Her heart. The picture of the man she had shared life with for so many years.

Her mental picture showed a gray-haired

man. His hair, once so thick, was now thin and wisping. His once full, tanned cheeks now were seamed and soft with the caress of old age. He was not as tall as he used to be. His grandsons, with their straight backs and broad shoulders, seemed to tower above him. Lizzie often wondered if he really had been as tall as she had once thought or if each new generation was just a little bigger than the one that preceded it.

But he still had the same sparkle of amusement in those eyes, the same gentle, yet mischievous smile that had first won her heart so many years ago. She would always carry that picture of him in her heart. A wooden box or a mound of earth would not hide it from her.

Subconsciously her hand reached up to finger her pearls.

She had to find some way to say goodbye but she didn't know how. Couldn't find any

words—and her feelings were all knotted up inside, like a strangling fist around her heart, threatening to squeeze the life from her. Duncan was gone. She still couldn't believe it. Couldn't accept it, even though she knew it to be true. How would she ever go on without him? Did she even want to? She felt so numb. Drained.

And then she lifted her eyes to the trees beyond. The family stood in the shade from the afternoon sun, anxiously shuffling about as they waited with concern while she said her final farewell to the man who had been a part of her for so many years. They were hers, those shuffling figures. Hers and Duncan's. Sons, daughters, grandchildren, great-grandchildren. They were her legacy of love. Her part of Duncan that she was allowed, by God's grace, to keep with her, even though he had been called on ahead.

"It won't be long," she whispered as the

tears began again to freely fall. "It won't be long. But I have to stay for now."

She swallowed. Tried hard to think of some good reason why she must remain behind. At length a thought came to her, and she grasped at it with all her might. "Have to wait to see just who this new great-grandchild will be", she told Duncan inwardly. "They say it's the last—this little number eleven—and I suppose they are right. They say they are getting too old to be getting up nights with babies. Couples plan their families now, you know. So this one—this little one—will be rather special. The last of another generation.

We won't be here to see the next generation grow and develop, Duncan," her silent communication continued. "Though I'd sure love to see a great-great-grandbaby or two. Could, too, you know. I'm only seventy-three and Marcie is already going on twelve."

She hesitated. "But I don't know. The way I feel today..."

She lifted her eyes again to the little crowd that was her family.

"They are waiting. They fret. You know how it is. Now they will never rest. With you gone they'll insist—well, I'm not ready to give up the farmhouse yet. With John farming the place there is no reason I can't stay on...."

She stirred and flushed slightly. She was glad that no one was nearby. Even though she was not speaking the words audibly, it would be thought strange—her talking to her departed husband. But how would she ever manage without Duncan to commune with? They had always talked over everything. Shared everything. Everything but his secret of the pearls. How had he kept that from her? She who had assumed she knew his every thought. She smiled. He had been so sweet about it. Her fingers tightened on his gift that rested gently against the front of her black mourning dress.

Lizzie caught herself up short. "I...I must stop...can't allow myself to talk like this," she scolded. "But it's just going to be so hard to...to think things...feel things and not want to share."

She lifted a handkerchief and dabbed at her eyes.

"It'll be all right. I'll...I'll just have to talk with God—even more."

Her thoughts changed. As did her inner words.

"Lord, I'm going to need you now—more than ever. You know...."

But she couldn't go on. There was no way to express what she was feeling. Her days and nights stretched endlessly before her—without Duncan. So lonely. She had no hope of making it through them on her

own. She would need to lean on God for strength to face them one at a time.

The waited-for baby arrived in June and seemed to awaken Lizzie from her long night of misty darkness. Life took on renewed interest and meaning with a little bundle to cradle and love. This little one is to be the last great-grandchild, Lizzie reminded herself, making her even more special. And added to that fact was the significant matter of her name. Pete and Heather called her Elizabeth in honor of her great-grandmother. Lizzie did not try to hide her delight.

From the beginning there seemed to be a special bond between the elderly woman and the tiny child. It was little Beth who switched the family's formal address from Great-grandmother to Nana. Heather had

corrected gently, trying to get the child to use the longer, more cumbersome title, but Beth didn't seem able—or willing—to say Great-grandmother. Lizzie just smiled. "I think she's on to something," she said with satisfaction. "Why have we burdened the others with that long name all these years?"

So Lizzie became Nana to all her off-spring, even her children. She liked the sound of the simple address. It was like a term of endearment.

Nana & Beth

"Can I stay with Nana?"

The question was asked frequently by Beth. There seemed to be nothing that she loved better than to spend time with her aging great-grandmother.

"Well, I don't know if—" began Heather.

"It's a wonderful idea—if you don't have other plans," Lizzie was quick to say.

Heather did not hesitate for long. "All right," she allowed. "But don't talk Nana into doing too much, and you mind your manners."

Beth just beamed. It was not hard to mind

her manners at Nana's house. Nana, though certainly not permissive, was not quite as strict about some things as her mother.

As soon as the car had left the farmyard, Beth bounced to a spot on the comfortable chair that she always claimed, folded her hands in her lap, and beamed at her great-grandmother. "What shall we do today?" she asked before her Nana could voice the familiar question.

Lizzie chuckled. The young child imitated her in everything.

"What would you like to do?" she responded. "Bake sugar cookies?"

Beth tilted her head, appearing to think deeply. "Maybe we should visit," she responded.

Lizzie chuckled again.

"Over tea," went on the small child.

"Over tea," Lizzie agreed and carefully lifted herself from her chair.

"I'll go get ready while you fix it," Beth, delighted, flung over her shoulder as she left the room at a forbidden run.

The dress-up trunk was kept in the closet in the back bedroom. Lizzie, carefully shuffling her way toward the kitchen, knew that's where Beth was headed. She would make the tea and prepare the plate of cookies while the child donned a hiked-up dress, flowing shawl, and out-of-date hat.

Beth was soon back. She looked smugly *elegant* as she clambered up onto a kitchen chair and settled in. "It's too cold this time to tea on the veranda," she informed her great-grandmother.

"Take tea," Lizzie corrected.

"Take tea?"

"We go for tea, serve tea, have tea, or take tea together. We don't just tea," Lizzie explained in a gentle voice as she poured the hot water into the teapot.

"Take tea," Beth repeated solemnly.

Lizzie placed the sugar cookies on a plate while the tea had a moment to steep. Then she poured from the big pot into a small pot that had already been half-filled with milk. The diluted tea was Beth's pot. Lizzie would enjoy the real thing.

Beth's eyes shone with her eagerness. She could hardly wait to get started.

She was about to pour out a cup when her head jerked upright.

"You should be dressed up too, Nana," she informed Lizzie.

Lizzie smiled. "Now, child, I don't think I wish to delve into that dress-up trunk," she replied good-naturedly. She eased herself onto her chair.

"Well—you could wear a hat," Beth suggested.

Lizzie thought about it. "I'll wear a hat—if you like," she responded.

Beth hopped down from her chair and ran for a hat for her great-grandmother. The one she brought had been mishandled and misshaped until it didn't sit well on Lizzie's gray hair—but she wore it, perched at an odd angle above her simply styled bun.

Beth studied her great-grandmother seriously. At length she spoke. "I know," she said with enthusiasm, "you should wear your pearls."

"Oh, not my pearls," Lizzie replied quickly. "They are much too special for playing dress-up."

"But you wear them lots," responded Beth, her voice sounding puzzled.

"Yes...yes, I do. Pearls are meant to be worn. It is good for their luster, they say."

"Then..."

"Because. They are special. I wear them on *special* days. On Sundays—when I go to church and have dinner with the family. On

family days. Birthdays. Anniversaries. Holidays."

"Weddings?" queried Beth as she prepared to pour her tea.

"Some weddings," agreed Lizzie. "But if it's a family wedding—like a granddaughter—then I let her wear the pearls instead."

Beth's blue eyes grew even larger.

"Will you let me wear them when I have a wedding?" she asked excitedly.

Lizzie smiled. She felt the tears threatening to spill. "Of course," she replied a bit huskily.

The pint-sized girl grinned and poured from her small teapot and carefully stirred in a spoonful of sugar. Two swallows emptied the tiny porcelain cup, and she reached for a refill.

Lizzie toyed with her own teacup as she looked at the beloved little face, at the shining blue eyes. "But first," she went on,

"I think you should know all about the pearls. About your great-grandfather. He was a wonderful man. I'm sorry you missed knowing him. You would have got on just fine—the two of you."

"Mama told me about him," the little girl said with a hint of sadness. "She said the pearls are priceless."

Lizzie nodded and watched as Beth helped herself to a cookie from the plate. The pearls *were* priceless.

Beth cocked her head to one side. "What's priceless, Nana?" she asked.

For one moment Lizzie struggled with an explanation. "Well—priceless means—you know what price means, don't you?"

Beth nodded. "It means how many monies something costs," she replied, nodding importantly.

"Yes," agreed Lizzie. "Well—when you add *less* to the word, that means without.

Without price. Price—less."

"You mean they cost *nothing?*" exclaimed Beth, a frown creasing her smooth brow.

"Well...no. It means—well it means that they cost so much that the money really can't be...be figured."

Beth's frown deepened. "Great-grandfather had *that* much money?" she exclaimed at length. "I didn't know he was rich."

"Oh, he wasn't rich," Lizzie quickly corrected. "Not like that. I mean—it wasn't the money that he paid for the pearls that makes them so...so special—though they did cost him dearly. But it wasn't the...the dollars. It was the...love. The sacrifice to save the money for their purchase—that is what makes the pearls so special. That is why they are priceless. I couldn't begin to—to even think of them as—to think of their worth in just dollars."

The frown left the little face. Beth

stirred another small spoonful of sugar into her milk-tea. "That's why you wear them on special days?"

Lizzie nodded, her eyes threatening to spill again. "That's why I wear them. To remind me of your great-grandfather's love."

"But you let other people wear them too?"

"On their wedding day," agreed the great-grandmother.

"To remind *them* of great-grandfather's love?"

"Yes, and to remind them that marriage takes love. It takes sacrifice. It takes working together and looking out for the best for each other."

Lizzie was sure that much of what she was saying was not understood by the small girl opposite her at the little kitchen table. But the day would come, and far too quickly, when the words would be understood.

She herself would reinforce them at every opportunity as the years went by. It was so important to have the right attitude, the right expectations, when one entered into a marriage relationship.

"I can hardly wait," said Beth pouring more tea into the tiny cup. "I can hardly wait until it's my turn to wear them."

Marcie, though the oldest, was not the first of the second generation to announce plans for marriage. She had chosen to seek a career and felt that being married might interfere with her ambitions. Inwardly Lizzie struggled with this new way of thinking, but she held her tongue. This generation saw things differently than young folk had in her day.

It wasn't just their thinking. It was

everything. They lived differently, dressed differently, talked differently. Sometimes Lizzie found it hard to understand their ways. Occasionally she had to hold herself in check. Some of the things they did, their way of going about things, didn't set well. She had to continually remind herself that so far—so far—none of them had rebelled. So far, they were still holding to their faith, to the beliefs she and Duncan had felt so important. For that she was deeply thankful. Yet it was hard at times not to try to impose her thinking about how those beliefs should be lived out in daily life.

Andrea was the first great-grandchild to announce her plans of marriage. The boy was an accounting student at the nearby university, and the young couple was excited about setting up housekeeping in a trendy apartment in the city. They were not going to have a traditional wedding. Just a few

friends and family. Weddings cost too much money, and their dollars would be more suitably spent on a honeymoon to Bermuda, Andrea explained. Her dress would not be long and white and veiled. That was a ridiculous expense. She was going for something that could be worn later—to parties or formal events.

Each time the family gathered, excited plans relating to the coming wedding filled the air. All the talk seemed foreign to Lizzie. She realized more and more just how much the world had changed.

It set her to thinking. At length she brought the matter up, determined to have her say before someone brought the discussion to her.

"I've done a good deal of thinking," she began as the women gathered in the kitchen after the Sunday meal. "Times have changed. Styles have changed. I know that I have talked a good deal about each of the family brides wearing the pearls." She took a deep breath and hurried on. "Well...that is to be *their* choice."

She could feel all eyes on her face.

"Each bride must determine whether...whether they feel the pearls are—what do they say—'me'? Isn't that the word? It's 'me'—or isn't 'me'? Well, I don't want anyone to feel they need to wear the pearls just to...to placate an old woman. They are there. For anyone who is pleased to wear them. But that will be the choice of each bride—by turn. If they decide that they wish them for the day—they need only ask."

She finished her speech and lowered herself carefully to a kitchen chair. She did not see the relieved look in the face of her granddaughter Claire who'd had countless arguments with the young Andrea. Now Claire would not have to make any awkward

explanations to her grandmother. Nor did Lizzie notice the triumphant look of Andrea, the bride-to-be.

Two weeks later Andrea stood before the minister in the family garden, the folds of ankle-length lavender tulle gently stirring against her slim figure. The neckline, though somewhat revealing in Lizzie's eyes, was ungraced by Nana's pearls, and she firmly told herself that it was all right. It was Andrea's choice.

Lizzie watched as three more family brides blushed their way through those special times known as wedding days. Each wedding was different. Each dress suited to the "me" who was the bride. Not once was the string of Nana's pearls spoken of—nor requested. Lizzie had them all to herself. She

wore them each Sunday, each special day, and at each of the weddings of her four great-granddaughters.

Marcie was still a holdout. Her career had soared. She had what she wanted and had no intention of spoiling things. Marilyn took the council of her older cousin and also sought a career in the city. Lizzie nodded, happy for their success, but inwardly she wondered about their choice. Who would be there for them in those days after the career? What memories would they have? But Lizzie said nothing about her feelings. She did not really understand this new generation.

Her daily prayer list grew longer and longer.

Beth and the Pearls

"Nana—I am getting married."

With the words, Beth threw herself in her great-grandmother's arms. Her eyes were glowing, her cheeks flushed.

Lizzie, who had slowly made her way to open the door in answer to the impatient rap, patted the slim shoulder, smiling and calm outwardly, but feeling strangely bereaved at the same time.

"I'll make some tea and you can tell me all about it," she managed to say. It was

more a stall for time than anything.

"I'll make it," offered Beth and released her great-grandmother. "You just sit."

Lizzie did not argue.

Soon they were having tea together. They no longer used the little cups or the two pots, the smaller for the child, the larger for the elderly woman. They no longer wore the silly old hats from the dress-up trunk. They were both adults now. Beth was a college senior.

Lizzie looked into the shining face and sparkling eyes.

"The young man you've been bringing home?" she asked gently, her voice cracking some.

Beth nodded, her large blue eyes intensifying with deep feeling.

Lizzie should have known. Should have seen it coming, but it had managed to catch her off guard. Somehow it seemed that her little Beth was so young. Little more than a child.

Lizzie liked the young man. In fact, she had taken to him immediately. There was no one that she would sooner see her Beth sharing a lifetime with—only it didn't seem real that her little girl was old enough to be a bride. She swallowed with difficulty. Who would "tea" with her now?

"Kevin—he seems like a fine young man," she managed to say. She even forced a wobbly smile.

"Oh, he is, Nana," responded Beth with exuberance, her voice full of love. "You know, from what you've told me—I think he's much like Great-grandfather."

Lizzie could not continue to meet the eyes. Not with her own filling with unwanted tears. She lowered her head and studied the small chip on the rim of her cup. She should discard it—but it was one of her favorites. Duncan had given it to her for her twenty-ninth birthday. Idly she wondered if he had already been saving then for the pearls....

The time of distraction gave her a few moments to reflect on Beth's words and to get her own feelings under control.

"Perhaps you are right," she agreed. She lifted her head again. "And if you are—you are blessed indeed. Your great-grandfather was a wonderful man."

Lizzie knew Beth had heard those words many times over the years. She was more sure of their truth than ever. And she thought she saw a new understanding of them in her great-granddaughter's eyes.

"Nana," Beth continued after a moment, seeming a bit nervous, even though they had never had reason to be uneasy with one another. "I have a...a rather large request. I know that it is hard for you to...to get

around. But I wondered if you would mind—if it would be too difficult for you—to come to the city with me to shop for my wedding dress?"

Beth stopped and took a deep breath, then hurried on. "I want to be sure that the neckline will...will show off the pearls to the best advantage."

Lizzie let the words sink in and then reached for her hankie. She could not stop the tears from flowing.

Beth seemed to misunderstand and reached out a hand. "I'm sorry," she whispered. "I didn't mean to—I can get a gown that I think will work and bring it here. I'll—"

"No. No, that's all right," Lizzie cut in quickly. "It's just...just—I am pleased that you still wish to wear them."

She patted the young girl's hand, stopped to wipe the tears and gently blow her nose.

"I just...thought...maybe they were so old-fashioned that even you—"

"Oh, Nana," said Beth with deep feeling. "I...I just couldn't even picture a wedding without them."

A wash of love swept over Lizzie. Beth had always been her special little soul mate. She would do anything for the girl. However, she was not up to a day of city shopping. But she did not need to be. Beth could purchase her gown with the pearls in hand.

"Take the pearls. It's not necessary for me to tramp about with you—hampering your shopping. Just take the pearls and try them with the dresses. I'm pleased that you want them. Really pleased. I had—well, I thought that maybe none of the great-granddaughters would want to wear something so out-of-date. I mean—things have changed so much that I...I don't know how to...to judge

things any more."

"Nana," Beth said softly. "Things haven't *really* changed. Family is still family. Love is still love. The other girls—they might live a little differently, but they are still trying to build homes. Love their husbands. Follow God."

Lizzie dabbed at her cheeks and nodded. Of course it was true. They were good kids. Good God-fearing kids. All of them.

"It's just that I'm...I'm more tied to the past," Beth said, and there was a chuckle in her voice. "Or maybe it's just the pearls. I've loved them ever since—ever since I can remember. As a little child I used to sit on your knee and be held close while I played with them. Remember? They were always there. Always a part of my Nana."

Lizzie threatened to cry again. Beth looked about to join her.

"We want a traditional wedding. Both of

us," Beth went on. "I think Kevin is almost as sentimental as I am."

Lizzie nodded. He was a fine young man, Beth's Kevin.

"Take the pearls with you," she said again with certainty.

Beth smiled. "As soon as I find just the right gown I will come model it for you—for your approval," she said, rising from her chair and placing a kiss on the wrinkled forehead.

"The pearls are in the top dresser drawer on the left. Take the blue box. I always keep them in their box when I'm not wearing them."

Beth went to get the pearls, and Lizzie idly poured another cup of tea for something to occupy her hands and thoughts.

"I will be very careful with them," Beth promised as she returned to the kitchen

with the box, the velvet now worn in spots from the many years of handling.

"They are insured," Lizzie found herself saying—just as Duncan had said so many times over the years.

But Beth stopped just before she left the kitchen and looked at her great-grandmother with much love and understanding. "One can't properly insure something that is priceless," she said softly, and then she was gone, closing the door gently behind her.

Beth modeled the new gown. The pearls lay gently against her fair skin and enhanced the luster of the satin. "The saleslady said that she had never seen such elegant pearls," she bubbled excitedly as she moved gracefully toward the chair where her great-grandmother sat, cane still in her hand.

Lizzie could not help but feel pleased that the clerk had noticed the worth of the pearls, even though she could not possibly have guessed their real value. Her eyes grew damp. But it was more than the pearls that brought the tears. Beth's radiance as she swung around to face her great-grandmother, eyes shining, satin skirts swishing as they gently brushed the wooden floor, made her breath catch in her throat. She would make a lovely bride, her little Beth. Kevin was a blessed young man.

The gown had been chosen with great care. The neckline was neither too revealing nor too high to show the pearls to the best advantage. Lizzie managed to voice her approval. "You have chosen well, dear," she said, brushing tears quickly away with a cambric hankie.

"You like it?"

"You bring out the best in the gown,"

answered the elderly woman.

"Oh, Nana," said Beth with a gentle laugh, "you have always been my best cheering section." And she bent to place a kiss on the withered cheek.

Straightening, she lifted the train of her gown and swung around one more time for her great-grandmother's pleasure. It reminded Lizzie of when Beth was a little girl, spinning in the dress-up clothes from the trunk in the far bedroom.

"I hate to take them off—the dress *or* the pearls," the young bride-to-be admitted, reaching up to unclasp the necklace. "I feel so...so wonderful in them. But I guess I must. Mama says the day will arrive all too soon."

Lizzie smiled. "Well, it better," she said lightly. "We don't have all that much time. You know I'm nearing my ninety-third birthday."

"Oh, Nana," scolded Beth softly as she

kissed the top of her white hair and returned the pearls to their box. "Don't even tease about such things," she said as she went to put the box back in the dresser.

Lizzie let the words go. But all the same she wondered. She had not confessed to her family, but she had been feeling strange lately. Little bouts of dizziness. Of breathlessness. She couldn't really put the feelings into words, but she sensed something. Something different about how her body was responding. She did so want to see her Beth walk down the aisle. She hoped that God would grant her another few months.

The News

"Mama. Mama."

Lizzie pushed back the hand-made patchwork quilt and fought for consciousness. Who could possibly be calling her at this hour? What could be the reason?

At once she thought of Andrea. The young woman was expecting the first great-great-grandchild—but she was not due for another two months. Besides, they had never awakened her before in the night to tell her of a birth in the family. She must be dreaming.

"Mama."

The voice persisted. Lizzie struggled to make sense of it. She reached up and brushed at the loose gray hair that had spilled about her face, trying hard to focus her thinking and her sleep-dimmed eyes.

"Mama. Mama—I'm sorry to waken you like this."

She recognized the voice then. It was John who stood near her bed. Her son. Lizzie still could not think of her boy as an elderly man—even though he was about to become a great-grandfather.

"What is it?" she managed, struggling to a sitting position.

John reached out a big hand and brushed back her hair. "I'm sorry," he said again and eased his frame to a sitting position on the edge of her bed. "I hated to come at this hour but—"

He did not go on, and Lizzie let her eyes

drift to the window where the first flush of a new day was gently caressing the eastern sky. In the garden a robin called.

"There's been an accident," he managed, his voice husky with emotion.

Lizzie felt weak. She would have dropped back to her pillow had not John been supporting her. The whole world seemed to spin around her. She could not even speak to ask the questions to which she must have answers. John seemed to understand.

"Beth," he said as gently as he could.

The one simple word jerked her fully awake with its harsh reality. Not Beth. Not her Beth. Beth was to be a bride in two weeks' time. It couldn't be.

"It's pretty bad," John carefully went on. She had to know.

She just looked at him blankly, willing the whole thing to be a horrible dream. She let her eyes search out the window again. A

soft breeze rustled the frills of the lace curtain.

"How bad?" she managed, though her mouth felt dry, her throat constricted.

"She has a few face cuts. Nothing serious. A broken arm. Maybe some internal injuries—they don't know yet. And...they are worried about her...spine."

"Oh, dear God, no," pleaded Lizzie, allowing the tears to come. John pulled her close to comfort her, and she wept against his heavy flannel shirt.

"Poor Heather and Pete," Lizzie said when she could speak again.

John nodded. "They are at the hospital with her now."

"What about Kevin? Poor boy."

"I don't know if they have reached him yet."

Lizzie thought of the shock in store for the young man. He was such a fine young fellow. Her tears flowed again.

"She's in the County General," John went on. "There is some talk of taking her to the city by air ambulance."

Then it was more than *pretty bad*. They could lose her.

Lizzie pulled away and tugged at the covers. John rose to his feet, and she threw back the blankets and swung her flannel-draped legs over the side of the bed.

"I must go to her," she said with urgency.

"Mama? One of the girls will be right over to stay with you. I'm not sure it's wise—" began John but she cut him off quickly.

"Well, I am," she said frankly.

"You know it's hard for you to walk. Those hospital corridors stretch on for miles," John argued further.

"Then get me one of those wheelchairs they have sitting all over the halls," she said with finality.

He seemed to concede, though she knew he still thought she was being foolish. Stubborn.

She turned to the dresser drawers to withdraw undergarments, and John moved toward the bedroom door.

"I'll be ready in a few minutes," she informed him. "You go on out and put on the coffeepot."

She wasn't sure who would drink the coffee, but she figured John needed something to do while he waited.

❧

There was the proverbial good news and bad news awaiting them. The doctor assured them that Beth would make it. Lizzie felt a wave of warm thankfulness wash over her body. But his next words brought her a chill again. The face would heal with little scar-

ring. The internal injuries did not appear to be life-threatening, but they were concerned about the spinal injury. Of course, all the testing had not yet been done, but there may have been serious damage....

Lizzie turned away from the slightly offi-cious-sounding words. She did not wish to hear them.

"May I see her?" she asked when the doc-tor paused for breath.

It was not really a request, even though it had been worded as one, but the tone of voice clearly indicated that Lizzie had every intention of seeing her great-granddaughter.

"Certainly," said the professional man in the white coat. "Her parents are with her. I wouldn't stay long. She has been given a fairly heavy sedative. She won't be ready to talk just now."

John got permission to use one of the wheelchairs, and Lizzie settled herself for a

ride down the long hall, her purse tucked in her lap and her cane propped up beside her. It seemed to take forever to reach Room 1253.

When they arrived at the door, Lizzie steeled herself for what they would find on the other side of the drawn white curtain. But still she was not prepared to see Beth as they found her when John pushed her chair near. The slender young figure lay draped with white linen, tubes attached in several places, machines monitoring each beat of her heart, each intake of breath. Her face was so pale it seemed to blend into the whiteness of the pillow on which her head rested. Lizzie noted two gauze bandages and guessed that they covered the facial cuts.

At the sound of the approaching chair, Heather looked up and with a little cry of "Oh, Nana," she flung herself at Lizzie and cried for many minutes. Pete stood by.

Awkward. Blinking. Fighting for control. And all the while the girl on the bed slept on. Still. Silent. Untouched by the drama of the room.

"What happened?" asked Lizzie when at last they were able to speak.

Pete answered. "She swerved to miss a deer. Link was right behind her on the road. Saw it all happen. Her little car rolled. If he hadn't been there to give help..." He let the rest of the sentence go unfinished. Lizzie knew how it would have ended. She was

thankful that the neighbor man had shared the road.

Lizzie moved awkwardly out of the chair and made her way to the side of the bed, her cane making a thump, thump on the tiled floor. Beth's hand felt cool and limp as Lizzie took it in her own.

If only she could make a trade. Could offer her own body in place of—but that was a foolish thought. Her old body was worn out from years of living.

"As soon as she is stabilized they plan to take her to the Big Hospital."

Everyone in the area called the city hospital the Big Hospital. To say that one had been sent there was to admit that the situation was serious. Lizzie knew of several who had gone to the Big Hospital and not come home. The words made her shudder with apprehension and fear.

"Have you contacted Kevin?" John

asked.

"They had an awful time tracking him down at that university," Pete said, "but he's on his way now."

"Poor boy," said Heather and pulled a fresh tissue from the box on the little table.

"Mama," said John, pushing the wheelchair a little nearer to where she stood as his suggestion that she place herself in it again. "I think you should go now. You can come back when—"

But Lizzie was wondering when she would see her Beth again. It was a long trip to the Big Hospital. A trip she was not happy to make. But if Beth was to be there, then she would go. She knew that.

She squeezed Beth's limp hand. "I'm leaving now, sweetheart," she whispered. "But I'll be back. I'll be back—no matter where they take you. You hang on now. You hear." And she squeezed the hand again.

Questions

The next weeks were some of the most difficult of Lizzie's life. The wedding date came—and went. Beth stayed at the Big Hospital for the best—or worst—part of two long months, and Lizzie traveled to see her with John and Cecily once a week during that time.

It was a discouraging time. The test results were not favorable and brought little hope that Beth would ever walk again. There were many tears and a multitude of pleading prayers—and a steady stream of

bold words intended as offerings of encouragement. Lizzie wondered if some of the words were said in pretense. Not lies to one another—or Beth. Just pretending—like a child at play. Let's pretend it's all going to turn out right. Let's pretend your spine will heal itself. Let's pretend you'll be able to walk again—down the aisle, around

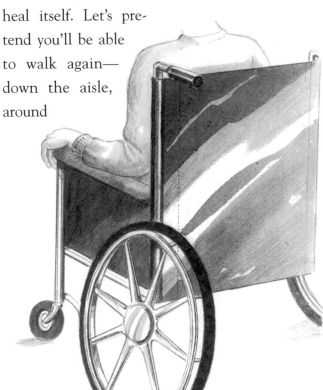

your kitchen, to the baby's room to care for the infant's needs—to walk—and be—a normal bride, wife, and mother. Let's pretend. Lizzie wearied of the pretense. She wished they would all just hush. Would face the facts honestly. Would stop the rush of light, meaningless words concerning the bright future. And then one day as Lizzie knelt before the Lord—in attitude only— her bad knee no longer allowed her to prostrate herself—a little miracle took place. She was gently reminded that God was God.

"You speak of love," a small voice whispered. "How much do you think I love you? How much do you think I love Beth?"

It had not been an audible voice. Not a spoken word. But an inner communication. Lizzie could not have explained it. Nor could she have denied it.

She shook her head. "Lord," she argued

silently. "I have no doubt of your love."

"My power, then?"

"No. Oh no. Not your power. I know of your power. I have felt your power. Seen your power at work. Have read of your power—over and over." Lizzie fingered the Bible in her lap. The Bible that spoke of many miracles.

"Then what is troubling you?" came the same gentle voice.

Lizzie thought—long and hard and ended by shaking her head in confusion. "I'm not sure," she replied honestly.

"Then leave it to me," the voice came quietly but with great strength and clarity.

The tears began to trickle down the aged cheeks. Of course. Of course. It was the only sensible thing to do.

"Does this mean you will heal her, Lord?" she quizzed, the thought too awesome for her to even grasp.

"My child," came the voice once more, and it was filled with love—and patience—yet just a hint of reproof, as though reassuring a needlessly fretting child. "I love Beth. I will do what is best."

The tears flowed freely then. How foolish she had been not to trust God fully. Of course He would do what was best. Lizzie laid aside her inner struggles and rested in that love. With her faith strengthened, her prayers became more intimate. More earnest.

Beth was moved back to the County Hospital to begin therapy. Therapy. It sounded like such a good word. Like *bandage* or *ointment*. Something that would fix things up again. Bring healing. "She's in therapy" were the words the whole family used to inform folks that things were now on the upward swing.

But were they?

Even Lizzie, with her newly discovered level of faith, wondered. "Why don't they forget the therapy and just leave it to God?" she often thought. And then she admitted that therapy might be part of God's plan also, and she learned to relax and even encourage Beth in her extremely slow, painful, and tedious daily workouts.

But in her humanness, she couldn't help but worry some. Beth's progress was so slow. How long would it take before the wedding would be able to take place? Would she, Lizzie, be there to see her girl wear the gorgeous gown, the string of pearls resting gently against the cream of her neck? She wondered.

She could no longer deny it. There was something strange going on with her heart.

She still had not mentioned it to the family. They had enough worries at the present. Besides, one could not hope to live forever. Not on this earth. And there were times when she longed to go. Ached for the beauties of heaven, the release from arthritic pain and lonely nights. Longed to see Duncan again. She was often torn between staying to urge Beth on and leaving to be in a far better place.

Well, it was all in God's hands. He loved. He would do what was best.

They found Beth crying. It caught them all by surprise. Beth had been so brave. So trusting. She had often been the one to dry their tears—to make little jokes that brought the laughter. And here she was, her shoulders shaking with convulsive sobs.

The nervous, exchanged glances clearly expressed their concern and helplessness. Then Lizzie took a deep breath and nodded for John to push the wheelchair up to the bed. With another silent nod she motioned the others from the room. She heard the door close gently as they left as though on tiptoe.

Lizzie said nothing. Just reached for the now-frail hand and held it tight while she prayed for wisdom. Her own tears were falling.

"Oh, Nana," Beth cried when she was aware of who her visitor was and had man-

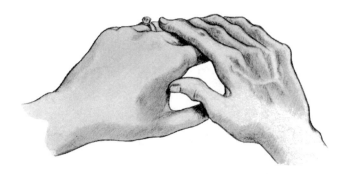

aged to wriggle to a position where she could wrap her arms around the frail little woman beside her.

They wept together.

After the storm had passed they shared the tissue box from the bedside stand, still not speaking.

It was Beth who spoke first. "It's not working," she said with finality.

Lizzie looked into the blue eyes, wet and red from tears. She did not answer.

"The therapy," Beth went on in explanation. "It's not working. I'm no better now than when I started."

"Is that what the doctors say?" asked Lizzie quietly.

"The doctors." Beth's voice held exasperation. "They say whatever they think you want to hear."

"Not really," Lizzie argued truthfully, stroking the hand she held. "They have been very honest and up-front about your chances of walking again. They know that we wanted to hear that everything would be fine in no time."

Beth seemed to think about that. At length she nodded.

"So—what do they say?" Lizzie probed again.

Beth swallowed hard, blinking back further tears. "They say—there has been *some* improvement."

"Some?"

Beth nodded.

"But not as much as you had hoped?"

Beth shook her head. "Hardly any," she said with disappointment. "Not as I see it."

"Have the doctors given up, then?"

"Oh no," Beth quickly cut in. "They want me to keep trying and trying—"

"And you aren't trying?" asked Lizzie frankly.

Beth looked shocked. "Of course I try."

There was irritation in her voice. Lizzie had never heard her speak in such a manner before. Especially not to her great-grandmother. She said nothing in response. Just continued to stroke the hand.

"It's hard, isn't it?" Lizzie said at last.

Beth nodded, needing another tissue.

There was silence for many minutes. At last Lizzie broke it.

"You know we are all praying for you."

Beth nodded mournfully.

"You know God loves you. In fact, He reminded me of that just the other day. 'I love her,' He assured me. 'I will do what is for her good.' That's a wonderful promise—don't you think?"

Beth nodded again, her eyes fastened on Lizzie's face.

"I love you, too," said the great-grandmother in a hushed voice. "I love you so much that I would never, never have let this happen to you—if I could have prevented it."

"I know," whispered Beth, biting her trembling lip.

"But God loves you even more. He loves you so much that He *did* allow it, because somehow...somehow He knew it would be for the good—for even your good. Now, I can't see how that could be, but He does. He does."

Lizzie hesitated, then said slowly, "The older I get, the more I realize that this life is so...so temporary compared to...to eternity. God is wise. Wise enough to chip away the unnecessary—so He can shape the immortal. What I'm trying to say, dear, is that God is more concerned with making us like Him, with making us holy than with making us happy."

She stopped again. It was a hard lesson.

Being shaped and molded. But she had confidence in God, first of all, that He would do His work in her and through her. And confidence in Beth. Confidence that she would get it worked through in time. And all of them—all of them would do some growing as they leaned on God for His help to face this tough time.

"He will work it all out. I believe that," Lizzie went on. "We can trust Him. That is what gets me through every day. I pray that it will help to get you through the days, too. The pain—the therapy—the disappointments. You just hang on to that trust. Do you hear? Hang on to that."

"Oh, Nana," sobbed Beth, wrapping her arms around the elderly woman and holding her close. "I don't know what I'd ever do without you." She clung to Lizzie and sobbed against the black-coated shoulder.

Lizzie held her and patted her. Her own

eyes clouded with tears. "Soon—perhaps very soon, you will need to learn about that, too, my dear," she thought. "But God will see you through that time as well."

The Legacy

*B*eth tried very hard over the next weeks of therapy, but even the most optimistic of the doctors had to admit the progress was slow. It was finally conceded by the medical attendants that it appeared the girl would not walk again. The news reached the ears of Lizzie, and she promptly rang up John and asked for a ride to the hospital room.

She expected to see Beth in tears again, but she was not. In fact, the pale, stoic face brought more pain to Lizzie's heart than the former flood of tears.

She nodded for John to place the wheel-chair close to the side of the bed and took a deep breath. Beth reached out for her great-grandmother's hand and attempted a smile. It was lopsided and uncertain.

"How are you, dear?" asked Lizzie, her rheumy eyes trying to penetrate the feelings of the girl on the bed before her.

"They are going to let me go home," Beth said, and there should have been some triumph—some pleasure in the statement—but there was not.

Lizzie nodded. "How do you feel about that?" she pressed.

Beth sighed, and for just a moment her gaze drifted away. Lizzie was sure that the tears would spill—but they didn't. Beth blinked them back with determination and turned toward her great-grandmother.

"I suppose—it's good," she replied.

"Suppose?"

"It'll be a real burden for Mama," answered Beth with a little quiver in her voice.

"Yes," agreed Lizzie, pushing her heavy coat back from her shoulders. "It will be that."

There was no use denying it.

For a moment there seemed to be nothing more to say. Lizzie reached down for the little bundle that lay in her lap. "I brought you something," she informed the girl.

Beth's face did not light up. There was scarcely a response at all.

Lizzie fished around in the interior of the bag and withdrew a blue box. She gently placed it in her lap and rubbed a bare spot on the velvet with her finger.

Beth's eyes opened wide. "The pearls?"

Lizzie nodded and quickly went on in a rush of words. "I'm hoping it won't be too

long until the Lord takes me home," she said gently but directly. She studied Beth's shocked face for a moment before she hurried on. "Don't be alarmed. When one gets my age, well... Some days I can hardly wait to go. This old body gets harder and harder to deal with. Most nights I can't sleep and most days I can't stay awake. Everything seems backward to what it used to be. I'm tired, my dear. Just plain tired."

She hesitated. It was the first time during this visit that tears threatened. "Besides," she went on, "I'm getting more and more lonesome for your great-grandfather. He was a wonderful man." She sighed deeply at the phrase she had thought and spoken so many times over the years. "So—I wanted to be sure that you have these—to go with your dress."

She looked up, the box now in her outstretched hand. Beth was crying, tears running freely down her cheeks.

"Oh, Nana," she sobbed. "I've already lost Kevin. I can't bear the thought of...of losing you, too."

"What do you mean?" asked Lizzie more sharply than she intended.

For a few moments the girl could not answer, but when she gained control she said, "Last night I told Kevin that the wedding was off."

"*You* told Kevin?"

She nodded.

"And what did Kevin say?"

A fresh burst of tears. "He is so...so stubborn. He...he refused to listen."

"So Kevin still wants to get married?"

"He says he does."

"And you don't believe him?"

Beth shook her head. "I don't see how...? How could he? Marry an invalid? What kind of life would that be? He's training to be a

doctor. He needs to be free to pursue his career. He needs a wife who—"

"A wife he can love," finished Lizzie. "One who loves him. Do you still love him, Beth?"

"Of course I do. How could I *not* love him? He's been so patient—so sweet."

"So why did you tell him that you can't marry him?"

"Nana—I'll never be able to walk down the aisle. Don't you see—?"

"Is that what you told Kevin?"

She nodded.

"And what was Kevin's answer?"

Unexpectedly, Beth smiled through her tears. "He said, 'Fine—I'm strong enough to carry you,' " she responded.

It was Lizzie's turn to smile.

"But I want to walk," argued Beth. "I don't want to be carried. Not down the aisle—not through life."

"Did you tell Kevin that?"

Beth nodded.

"And—?"

"He said, 'Well—I guess there's nothing to do but get you walking, then.' Nana, he...he just refuses to be realistic. He...he won't give up."

"Love is like that," Lizzie whispered.

"But I can't do that to him. I can't."

Lizzie took the girl's hand and caressed it gently. She spent many moments in deep thought and prayer before she spoke, but when she spoke her voice was firm. Sure. "As I see it," she said, "the only thing that you are *doing* to Kevin is refusing to trust him to know—how he feels—what he really wants. To return his love. Refusing to allow him to love you." She hurried on before the girl could voice a protest. "There are many helps now for a person who—who cannot walk. Wheelchairs"—she tapped the

side of the chair she was sitting in—"walk-
ers, canes, fancy straps and things—lots of
things."

She stopped her flow of words, hoping—
and praying that Beth was letting them sink
in. Then she took a deep breath and continued. "It is just your legs that aren't working,
Beth. Your heart is still intact. Can't you
see? Kevin loves *you*—not the fact that you
could once walk—and run. He loves you.
The real Beth in there. And that real
Beth—she is not wasted—like your legs.
She has grown. I've seen it happen. I've seen
the courage. The faith. It has grown. It has
responded to the *spiritual* therapy that has
been going on in your life. You're stronger
now than ever. You...you have almost...
almost learned to trust—completely. Only
this one—this one thing is holding you
back. Why, Beth? Why can't you trust God
in this too? Why can't you believe that you

can be just the wife that Kevin needs? That his life with you might make him into a better man? A better doctor?" Lizzie paused to search the eyes staring into hers. "Now, I don't pretend to understand any of this. But God does. I know that. And someday—perhaps even sooner than we dare to think—someday we will understand it too."

Lizzie hesitated—then again handed the velvet box to her great-granddaughter. This time Beth accepted the gift, the tears streaming down her face. She pulled the blue box close against her chest, as though she needed to cling to it.

Lizzie let her cry for several minutes before she spoke again. Her voice was soft, filled with emotion. "You remember—you once said that your young man—your Kevin—is much like your great-grandfather? Well—I think you are right. So right. You have been blessed, Beth. Blessed with the love of a wonderful man."

Beth sniffed, smiled crookedly, and reached for her Nana. They held each other a long time, rocking back and forth as they did when Beth was a little girl.

"Now—do I need to have someone call up that young man of yours and tell him to come—?" began Lizzie, pushing her gently back against the pillows.

But Beth was shaking her head, a smile lighting her face in spite of the tears still on her cheeks. "No," she said. "No, he said he'd be back. He said I'd made a promise and he was holding me to it. He said we weren't giving up. That, whatever happened, we'd face it together. He'll be back."

Lizzie smiled.

"And I'll wear your pearls, Nana," Beth went on. "I may have to tie up the skirts of my gown so they won't get all tangled up in the wheelchair—but I'll wear your pearls.

And we'll do it soon—just like Kevin wants. You'll have them back in your dresser drawer before you know it."

Lizzie stirred, then spoke. "I don't want them back. I want you to keep them. They are yours now. You're the one that I want to leave them with. I don't want anyone fussing over them—wondering how to share equally. They're the only thing I've got that's of any value."

Beth smiled and spoke in a teasing voice. "I thought you said their worth wasn't in the money value? Remember?"

"It's not," Lizzie agreed quickly. "It's not. Not their *real* worth—but you and I both know that the world sees it in quite another light. They *are* worth money, you know. We can't deny that fact. But it's the love— the sacrifice—that gives them their special value."

She stopped and looked into the blue

eyes of her great-granddaughter. "But I think you understand that—more than anyone, now."

Beth nodded. Solemnly. Thoughtfully. "Yes," she said. "I think I finally do."

Homegoing

Four days later John found her, still in her bed. The coroner's report stated that Lizzie had gone in her sleep. In stunned grief, the family could not believe that she was taken from them so quickly. Without a warning. Without a goodbye.

Beth's "Why, God? Why *now?*" whirled through her thoughts and emotions. After the discussion with Nana, she had renewed the wedding plans. Kevin had promised to be patient. To give her as much time as she

felt she needed to prepare herself—physical-ly—emotionally. She was beginning to make the adjustments in her thinking about her trip to the altar. But when the news came about Nana, the fact that she would not be there to share the special day brought deep pain. In her grief Beth at first wondered if she would be able to go through with their plans. Would the day that she had looked forward to now bring her more pain than joy?

And then she remembered the words her Nana had spoken. She was anxious to go Home, she had said. She was lonely. She was in pain. She was tired. Was it fair to wish her back? Gradually Beth was able to release her. Able to trust God. Able to acknowledge that God in His wisdom—and love—does *every-thing* right.

But the emptiness—the big hollow spot that her great-grandmother had left

behind—would be there for a very long time.

Beth waited in the wide foyer, her long white gown flowing out behind her. Her puffed veil secured in place. The string of Nana's pearls accentuating the elegant bodice of her gown. She shamelessly patted her eyes dry with Nana's favorite cambric hankie.

"God," she whispered, "I miss her so much. Even more today than...than usual. It's just so...hard to...be without her." The hint of a smile touched her lips as she glanced down at herself. "She would have been so pleased."

She was walking. No, not really. She was moving—in a clumsy way. Shuffling. Lunging. But she was not in a wheelchair. She would not have to be carried, though

her gait was unsteady, awkward. And she would not be able to take her father's arm because both of her hands would be fully occupied with her support aids. But he would be there at her side, ready to steady her should the need arise.

Still—she was mobile—in a way—though she had much mechanical help hidden beneath the folds of her bountiful skirts. Help, that barring a miracle, she would always need. Kevin, with his knowledge and influence, had obtained the best possible assistance for her uncooperative limbs. With the help of all the straps and harnesses and the use of the walking aids, she could move again. It was not a pretty picture, her jerking, lumbering gait, but Kevin seemed pleased that she was actually moving on her own.

Kevin! He was waiting for her down at the altar.

Beth blinked away tears and lifted her face to where the stream of light from the stained-glass windows splashed reflected colors on the cream ceiling.

She did not know how it worked. If her Nana was still—connected, somehow. Though she felt her presence there. In her heart. Nana's love—and influence on her life.

She whispered a little prayer, "God—thank you—thank you for giving me Nana for all those years." She paused, then continued, and there was pain yet pleasure that flooded her heart. "Thank you for her...her gift to me."

Oh, it wasn't so much the pearls, though she wore the beautiful necklace with pride. It was the love. The love—and the lessons in faith. Nana had taught her so much. Had given so much.

Beth hesitated. The glowing stream

through the window seemed to brighten.

"And thank you, God...for...teaching me what love really is."

She took a deep breath, gave her father a shaky smile, and nodded that she was ready to go join her Kevin—just as the first note of the Wedding March rose jubilantly from the church organ.